W9-AAO-946

For Adam and all children
who love adventure
KH

To Vitti with love
HC

Text copyright © 1990 by Katharine Holabird
Illustrations copyright © 1990 by Helen Craig

Published by Clarkson N. Potter, Inc., a Random House company,
201 East 50th Street, New York, New York 10022

Originally published in Great Britain by ABC in 1990

CLARKSON POTTER, POTTER, and colophon are trademarks of Clarkson N. Potter, Inc.

Printed and bound in Hong Kong by Imago Services (HK) Ltd.

Library of Congress Cataloging-in-Publication Data
Holabird, Katharine.
    Alexander and the magic boat / [Katharine Holabird,
illustrated by Helen Craig].
        p.   cm.
    Summary: Alexander, a little boy with a big imagination,
takes his mother on a voyage in his magic boat.
    ISBN 0-517-58142-6 $11.95
    [1. Imagination — Fiction.   2. Mothers and sons — Fiction.]
I. Craig, Helen, ill.   II. Title.
PZ7.H689Aj 1990
[E] — dc20   90-7252
                                                          CIP

ISBN 0-517-58142-6
ISBN 0-517-58149-3 (GLB edition)

10 9 8 7 6 5 4 3 2 1

First American edition

Alexander
and the Magic Boat

Story by Katharine Holabird   Illustrations by Helen Craig

Clarkson N. Potter, Inc./Publishers NEW YORK

Alexander loved to imagine great adventures, and every day he thought up something new.

One day, his mother gave him a real captain's hat, and Alexander decided to become a fearless captain of the high seas. He made a boat out of two armchairs, and sailed off to explore faraway places. But it got lonely sailing the seven seas, and he wished that someone would come with him.

He wanted to invite his mother, but she was always very busy. Alexander's mother could do a million things, and Alexander wished that he could do everything as easily as she did. She could cook, climb trees, stand on her head and she could bandage bleeding knees very gently.

She could fix bicycles and she could glue broken toys back together. She knew all about computers and microscopes, and she loved singing operas in the shower. Best of all, Alexander's mother wasn't afraid of spiders, and if she found one she gave it to Alexander to keep in a jar.

Alexander wished that he could give his mother something special, too, even though she always said that his hugs and kisses were the best presents in the world.

Then one afternoon, Alexander's mother stopped working and sat down. "I've been busy all day," she said. "I think I'll just rest for a minute."

Alexander looked at his mother in surprise. Then he had an idea.

"You can rest on my magic boat," Alexander suggested. "I'll be the captain and take you across the sea."

Alexander put on his cap and pushed the two armchairs together again. He brought some peanut butter and bread, in case they got hungry, and took his spider for good luck.

His mother smiled and put up her feet, while Alexander jumped
to the deck to steer. Then off they sailed together, across the
deep blue sea.

"This is a magic boat," Alexander explained. "It can take you anywhere. Where would you like to go?"

Alexander's mother thought for a moment. "I always wanted to see the other side of the world," she said.

"Let's go!" shouted Alexander, as the magic boat sailed across the sparkling water.

They travelled past dancing dolphins and singing whales, past schools of flying fish and families of smiling seals. Alexander and his mother sang an opera with the whales. They splashed with the dolphins. They reached out to tickle two enormous green turtles that swam slowly by, while the magic boat sailed on and on, following the song of the sea all the way to the other side of the world.

"I think I see an island!" Alexander pointed in the distance.
"Let's explore," said his mother, shading her eyes.

No sooner had Alexander landed his boat
than three greedy pirates leaped out of
the shadows. "AH-HA! A perfect
boat for pirates!" They grabbed
Alexander and his mother.

"Help!" called Alexander's mother,
kicking one of the pirates on
the shin bone.

"OOOH!" shouted the pirate,
hopping on one leg.

Then Alexander took his spider out of the jar and wiggled it under the pirates' noses.

"EEEEK!" shrieked the pirates, who were terrified of spiders.

"Please don't let that horrible spider touch us!" they cried, falling to their knees. The pirates begged for mercy and promised to be good.

"We've been shipwrecked here—our boat has a terrible leak!" they wailed.

"My mother can fix it," said Alexander proudly, and his mother borrowed a hammer and banged their boat back together before they could say "Captain Hook!". Then Alexander made them all peanut butter sandwiches and the pirates swore they would be best friends forever.

When they had finished eating, the pirates clambered aboard their pirate ship and waved goodbye.

Then Alexander and his mother spent the afternoon digging for buried treasure. Alexander presented his mother with an old silver spoon and a long-lost key. They didn't even notice that the sky was turning dark and the sea was getting rough.

"A hurricane!" cried Alexander. "If the boat blows
away, we'll never get back!"

The magic boat was bucking and leaping
in the foam, and Alexander caught the
rope just before it broke away.

He jumped on board with his
mother and the boat
plunged into the storm.

Then Alexander steered the magic boat back through waves that were higher than houses and winds that whistled and roared. Thunder and lightning exploded in the sky, and the dolphins, seals and whales hid in the wild darkness of the sea.

But Alexander was
such a good captain
that his mother fell fast asleep until they were safely home again.

Alexander carefully tied up his magic boat before he climbed into his mother's lap.

His mother stretched and smiled. "Thank you for the trip to the other side of the world," she said. "You know a lot about the sea, and pirates too! Will you take me on your boat again?"

"Yes! But I still have one more present for you," smiled Alexander, and he gave his mother a very special hug and kiss.